THE BOXCAR CHILDREN®

BLUE BAY MYSTERY

Time to Read™

Time to Read™ is an early reader program designed to guide children to literacy success regardless of age or grade level. The program's three levels correspond to stages of reading readiness, making book selection straightforward, and assuring that when it's time for a child to read, the right book is waiting.

— Level — **1**

Beginning to Read

- Large, simple type
- Basic vocabulary
- Word repetition
- Strong illustration support

— Level — **2**

Reading with Help

- Short sentences
- Engaging stories
- Simple dialogue
- Illustration support

— Level — **3**

Reading Independently

- Longer sentences
- Harder words
- Short paragraphs
- Increased story complexity

Library of Congress Cataloging-in-Publication data is on file with the publisher.

Copyright © 2020 by Albert Whitman & Company
First published in the United States of America
in 2020 by Albert Whitman & Company
ISBN 978-0-8075-0795-7 (hardcover)
ISBN 978-0-8075-0797-1 (ebook)

Printed in China
10 9 8 7 6 5 4 3 2 1 WKT 24 23 22 21 20 19

Cover and interior art by Shane Clester

Visit the Boxcar Children online at www.boxcarchildren.com.
For more information about Albert Whitman & Company,
visit our website at www.albertwhitman.com.

THE BOXCAR CHILDREN®

BLUE BAY MYSTERY

Based on the book by
Gertrude Chandler Warner

Albert Whitman & Company
Chicago, Illinois

Grandfather had a secret.
The Alden children could tell.
Grandfather loved to plan
things for his grandchildren.
And Henry, Jessie, Violet,
and Benny loved surprises.

The children had once lived
in a boxcar.
It had been their home.
They had many adventures
in the boxcar.
Then Grandfather found them.

Now the children had
a real home.
But they still had plenty
of adventures!

One day, the children met
a man named Lars.
Lars was Grandfather's friend.
He'd had an adventure of his own.
Years ago, his boat got stuck
on an island.
Lars lived there for weeks.
Then he was rescued.

"You must have been scared!"
Benny said.

Lars nodded.

"I was, but now I want
to go back,
with friends."

Grandfather told the children
his surprise.
They were all going to see
the island!
"What about school?"
asked Violet.
"You will learn along the way!"
he said. "I have planned it with
your teachers."
But no one, not even
Grandfather, could plan for
the biggest surprise.

They flew to San Francisco.
Then they got on a ship
to the South Seas.
It was a long trip.
On the way, the children saw
all kinds of new things.
Then they read about them
in books.
"Boat school is fun!"
said Benny.

At last, the ship reached
the island.
The water was the bluest the
children had ever seen.
"We should call this Blue Bay,"
said Benny.
The children laughed.
They all knew how Benny
liked to name things.

On shore were two old huts.
It was where Lars had stayed
when he was on the island.
The children made beds with
palm leaves.
They cooked over a fire on
the beach.
For cups, they used big white
seashells.
It was almost like living in the
boxcar again.

In the morning, Jessie noticed something.

A box of crackers was open.

"Benny, did you eat a snack?" she asked.

Everyone knew how much Benny liked to eat.

But only Benny knew that he had not opened the crackers...

In the afternoon, Lars led
the children to a waterfall.
The water was as clear as the air.
Benny noticed a white seashell
on a rock.
"What a strange place for a
seashell," he thought.
"It looks like our cups."
But Benny did not tell the
others what he saw.

At night, the children
had fish stew.
Then from the dark,
they heard a voice.
"Hello, Peter!" the voice said.
It was not a voice the
children knew.

A bird flew up.
"Careful, Peter, it's hot,"
said the voice.
"The bird!" said Henry.
"Someone has taught it to speak!"
"But who?" said Violet.
At last, Benny spoke up.
"There's a mystery here!"

The next day, the children explored.

"This bay is good for swimming," said Lars. "The reef keeps it safe."

The water was as green as Blue Bay was blue.

"I know the perfect name," said Benny.

"Is it Green Bay?" asked Jessie.

"How did you know!" said Benny.

The children laughed.
They swam in the cool water.
They almost forgot about
their mystery.
Until…

"Over here!" Henry called.
There was a little boat
on the reef!
"*Explorer II*," said Grandfather.
"That ship went down
months ago.
A young boy went missing.
His parents have been looking
for him."
The Aldens looked at
one another.
Was there another person
on the island?

Days went by.

The children did not find any more clues to their mystery.

But they did learn many new things.

Henry weaved a basket.

Jessie made bowls from coconuts.

Violet drew new plants.

Benny caught new fish.

The children were having so much fun, they thought they would never want to leave.

One day, the children went
back to the waterfall.
Benny searched for the seashell
that looked like a cup.
The shell had moved!

Then Henry called,
"Over here!"
He had found a cave.
Inside was a bed, and dishes!
Someone *was* living
on the island!

Benny heard a noise
in the treetops.
One tree, then the next.
Benny followed the sound.
He ran and ran.
He was so interested in the
sound, he did not watch
where he was going.

Whoosh!

Benny slid down into a hole.

He was stuck.

Benny called out.

But it was not Henry or Jessie

or Violet who came to help.

It was a young boy.

His name was Peter!

Peter told the Aldens his story.

He was the missing boy from
Explorer II.

He had lived alone on the
island for months.

He had been watching
the Aldens.

"You took our crackers!"
said Benny.

Peter nodded, but he knew
Benny was not upset.

"Why didn't you say anything?"
Grandfather asked.

"I was afraid," said Peter.

"Then I saw how nice you were."

"Hello, Peter," a voice said.

It was the little bird.

The bird flew to Peter's arm.

"You taught her, didn't you?"
said Jessie.

Peter nodded.

"She kept me company,"
he said.

"But this place is much better
with friends."

Before long, the ship returned.
The children said good-bye
to Blue Bay.
They loved the island.
But they could not imagine
living alone like Peter had.
It was time to go home.

On the ship, Grandfather was
busy making a new plan.
The children stayed with Peter.
Peter ate and ate.
"I think I missed peanut butter
most," he said. "No, toast!"
"Careful, Peter, it's hot,"
the bird said.
Everyone laughed.

It was not until they reached land that they saw what Grandfather was planning…

And Peter found what he really missed most.

Keep reading with the Boxcar Children!

Henry, Jessie, Violet, and Benny used to live in a Boxcar. Now they have adventures everywhere they go! Adapted from the beloved chapter book series, these early readers allow kids to begin reading with the stories that started it all.

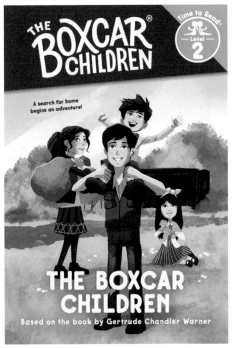

HC 978-0-8075-0839-8 · US $12.99
PB 978-0-8075-0835-0 · US $3.99

Four children.
One island.
Endless adventure.

SURPRISE ISLAND

Based on the movie *Surprise Island*
Based on the book by Gertrude Chandler Warner

HC 978-0-8075-7675-5 · US $12.99
PB 978-0-8075-7679-3 · US $3.99

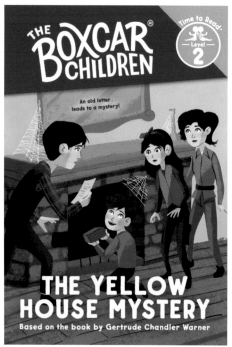

An old letter
leads to a mystery!

THE YELLOW
HOUSE MYSTERY

Based on the book by Gertrude Chandler Warner

HC 978-0-8075-9367-7 · US $12.99
PB 978-0-8075-9370-7 · US $3.99

HC 978-0-8075-5402-9 · US $12.99
PB 978-0-8075-5435-7 · US $3.99

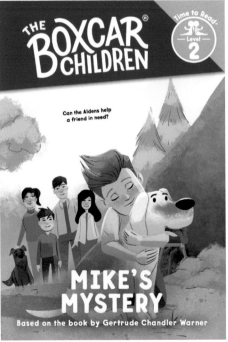

HC 978-0-8075-5142-4 · US $12.99

GERTRUDE CHANDLER WARNER discovered when she was teaching that many readers who like an exciting story could find no books that were both easy and fun to read. She decided to try to meet this need, and her first book, *The Boxcar Children*, quickly proved she had succeeded.

Miss Warner drew on her own experiences to write the mystery. As a child she spent hours watching trains go by on the tracks opposite her family home. She often dreamed about what it would be like to set up housekeeping in a caboose or freight car—the situation the Alden children find themselves in.

While the mystery element is central to each of Miss Warner's books, she never thought of them as strictly juvenile mysteries. She liked to stress the Aldens' independence and resourcefulness and their solid New England devotion to using up and making do. The Aldens go about most of their adventures with as little adult supervision as possible— something else that delights young readers.

Miss Warner lived in Putnam, Connecticut, until her death in 1979. During her lifetime, she received hundreds of letters from girls and boys telling her how much they liked her books.